ADVENTURES IN PENGUIN SITTING

First published in this format in 2015 by Curious Fox,
an imprint of Capstone Global Library Limited,
7 Pilgrim Street, London, EC4V 6LB
– Registered company number: 6695582
www.curious-fox.com

CAPG34399

Based on Tom and Jerry Tales
Adapted from a teleplay by Robert Ramirez
Text by Charles Carney
Illustrations by John Skewes and Stephanie Gladden
Originated by Capstone Global Library Ltd
Printed and bound in Slovakia by TBB

ISBN 978-1-782-02278-7
18 17 16 15 14
10 9 8 7 6 5 4 3 2 1

A CIP catalogue record for this book is available
from the British Library.

The National Literacy Trust is a registered charity no: 1116260 and a company limited by
guarantee no. 5836486 registered in England and Wales and a registered charity in Scotland
no. SC042944. Registered address: 68 South Lambeth Road, London SW8 1RL.
National Literacy Trust logo and reading tips © National Literacy Trust 2014
www.literacytrust.org.uk/donate

™

D1147058

One lazy afternoon, Jerry sat in front of his tiny TV as a cooking show chef celebrated Jerry's favourite cheese: "Mozzarella! Mozzarella! Mozzarella!" he cheered. "Even the way it rolls off your tongue is delicious!"

"MOZZ-AAA-RRRRRRRRRRRREL-LAA! AH! ZE AROMA OF ROME!"

But Jerry's wonderful thoughts of Mozzarella ended sharply as an announcer broke into the broadcast.

"Ladies and Gentlemen, we've just received word that a very dangerous penguin has escaped from the city zoo. He is considered cute and **EXTREMELY HUNGRY!** Shut your windows, lock your doors, and most of all — **HIDE YOUR REFRIGERATORS!**"

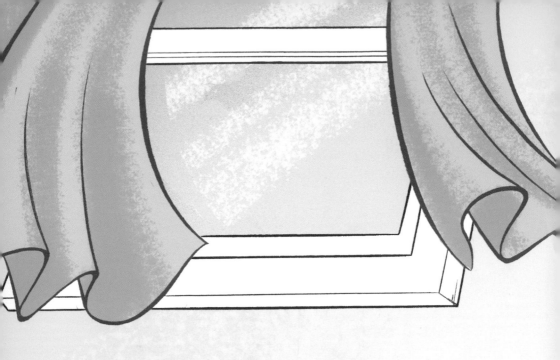

OH, NO! Jerry hurried into the living room. He closed the window. But as he struggled to lock the front door, the doorbell rang and the door flew open, knocking him to the floor.

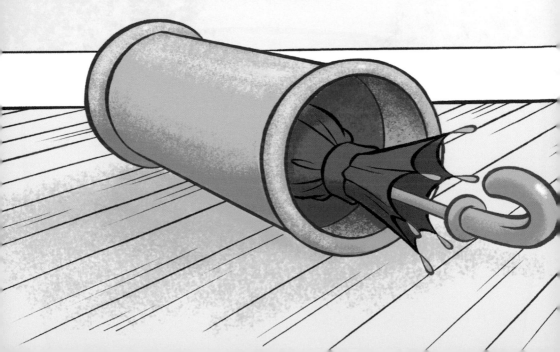

He looked up and saw,
outlined in the doorway,
the shape of a very menacing
...PENGUIN!

Jerry hid in an umbrella. When he finally got the courage to peek, he saw nothing but a cute little penguin. **HMMMM** ... *nothing dangerous here,* Jerry thought. The hungry penguin cheeped wildly and pointed at his mouth.

Before Jerry could explain that he didn't have any food, the penguin spotted the refrigerator and dashed to it. He went right past Tom who was savouring the last of his milk.

The little penguin threw open the freezer door, grabbed an armful of ice and waddled off.

Tom snatched the penguin from atop a hill of ice cubes and was about to teach him a lesson, but the penguin gulped down a cherry ice lolly and burped it into Tom's face, leaving him with a frozen red headpiece.

Jerry rushed to the penguin's rescue while Tom slipped on the icy floor and crashed face-first into the pile of frozen goodies.

"Thomas! What's going on down there?" hollered the Lady of the House. **UH, OH.** Guess who's going to get the blame? Tom hurried to put away the ice lollies, but was caught in a mess.

"Thomas! What are you doing in the freezer?" Tom
smiled meekly as he shut the freezer door. "This better
be cleaned up by the time I get back," she scolded. Tom
nodded, accepting the mop she shoved into his paws. Tom
looked at the mop, then at the mess, and shuddered at the
job ahead of him.

Jerry was delighted at Tom getting into trouble ...
until he noticed that the penguin was heading back to
the freezer.

Jerry told him off and had him wait while HE went
back to get more ice lollies. As Tom cleaned, Jerry quietly
opened the freezer door and lifted a grape ice lolly from
the tray, keeping a close eye over his shoulder. He turned
and ran straight into Tom's frowning face. **OOPS**. Jerry
smiled sheepishly and waved.

Jerry did his best to scatter, but didn't notice he was running on the thermostat. **DOWN, DOWN,** DOWN went the temperature in the freezer – a growing cold front spread through the house. Jerry got enough traction to launch himself into the living room with a furious Tom fast behind.

Jerry squeezed the little penguin into his mouse hole just as Tom caught up to them. **SLAM!** Tom's head was no match for the wall.

ACTIVITY!

can you find 5 hidden blocks of cheese?

PHEW! Jerry thought, clutching the last of the grape ice lollies. The penguin chomped it down in one bite and rubbed his tummy as he felt a burp forming. Tom peeked into the hole. **BLAAAP!** Tom got another sticky hairdo – this one purple! Tom puffed out an icy breath – now that was cold! In fact, everything seemed cold!

The haywire freezer had turned the entire house into a winter playground. **YIKES!** Six inches of snow blanketed the living room, with ice on the curtains, lamps and chandeliers!

As the penguin bolted from Jerry's mouse hole, Tom went after him.

ACTIVITY!

Find five things that don't belong in this scene.

But Tom didn't get far! The carpet was now covered in
a sheet of ice, and he ran in place like a dog on a waxed
floor. He slipped and took in a mouthful of freezing cold
air. Tom tried to growl but found his mouth full of icicles!

Meanwhile, the happy penguin lounged in the freezer, enjoying a variety of ice lollies. Jerry grabbed one away and motioned for the penguin to follow him. **OH, NO!** Tom was right behind him, but he couldn't stop on the icy floor. Luckily, a snow bank in the dining room stopped him.

ACTIVITY!

Can you find the two halves of lollies that do NOT connect?

Jerry was leading the hungry penguin away with the last of the treats. But Santa Cat grabbed the little penguin and plugged a cork in his beak to quiet him.
THINK FAST, JERRY!

Jerry grabbed a heavy frying pan and brought it down on Tom's foot. The pain sent him straight to the ceiling. As Tom landed, Jerry gave him a smack on the bottom with the frying pan, sending him into the freezer.

THAT'S QUICK THINKING!

The freezer shook as Tom shivered his way up and into the icemaker, which spat him out in little cubes.

THE CHASE WAS ON!

Jerry and the penguin scooted across the snowy floor. Tom shot after them using two pancake flippers for skis.

Faster and faster Tom raced, losing control, flying right past them, and crashing into the mouth of a stuffed moose. **CRASH! OUCH!** What could be worse? Just then the front door opened...

ACTIVITY!

One of the paths in the snow leads to the refrigerator. Can you show Tom the right path to take?

"Oh, Thomas! All this mess for an ice lolly?" the Lady of the House cried.

At the front door, the little penguin squeaked with delight as Jerry pulled him away.

Jerry and the little penguin shook hands as they stood in front of the penguin display at the City Zoo. It had been a **CRAZY** day, and they both had fun getting Tom into trouble. The penguin hopped over the fence and swam back to the other penguins. Jerry waved goodbye.

Jerry was resting on his little bed watching "The World of Cheese," when the doorbell rang. Jerry wasn't expecting anyone.

When he opened the door, he saw that the whole garden was full of penguins that had heard about the best place in town for ice lollies. You would think Jerry would be happy to have so many guests. Instead, he fainted.